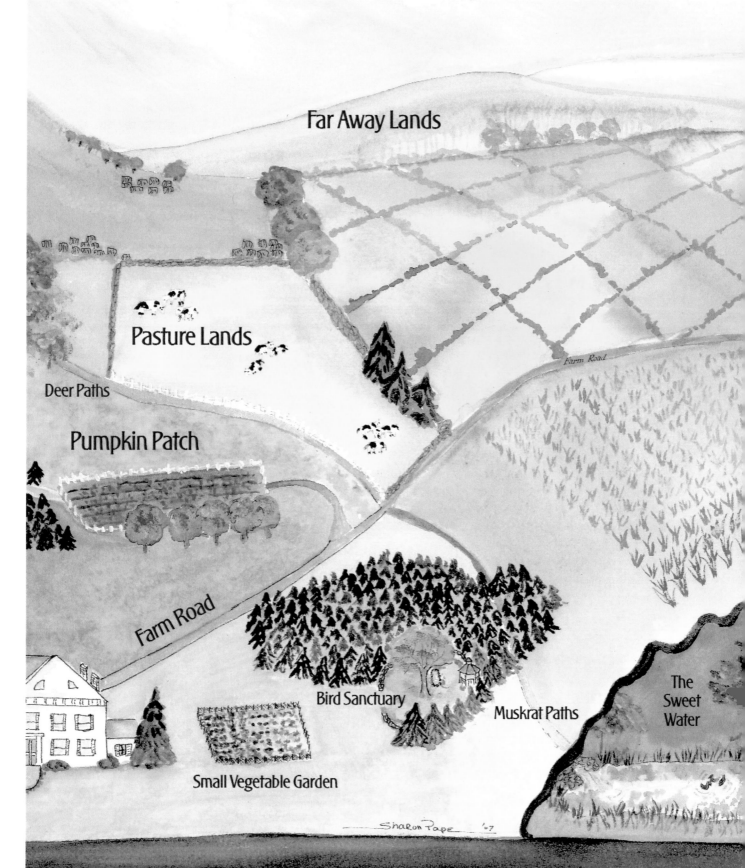

Far Away Lands

Pasture Lands

Deer Paths

Pumpkin Patch

Farm Road

Farm Road

Bird Sanctuary

Muskrat Paths

The Sweet Water

Small Vegetable Garden

Sharon Pape '07

ISBN 978-0-9797166-0-7

Printed and bound in the United States of America
Art direction/Layout: Frank Romeo, Camelot Media Group

Tails of
High Meadows

An Autumn Adventure

By Mary Stewart Granato

Illustrations by Sharon Pape

DEDICATION

To my loving husband, John, builder extraordinaire,

who gently nudged me when necessary and for his

unwavering support and belief in me.

To Order This Book:

Go to: www.bunnypufftailbooks.com

CONTENTS

Introduction
By Christina Yoshimura, Ph.D.

Get ready for some adventure! No matter where you are when you pick up this book, no matter what the time or the season, you'll soon find yourself in a countryside rich with autumn's beauty and bursting with colorful characters. You'll be off on a grand journey with Bunny Pufftail and Toddy the fieldmouse, and once you join their exploration you'll be amazed at all that you'll find and learn.

As a college professor and a researcher of families, I've had the chance to study many ways that families communicate, and many ways that they choose to spend their time. Often, families are choosing to engage in independent activities. One family member might be off at a soccer league, another might be on the Internet, and another might be watching television. It's great for families to find different things that make them happy. The problem comes in when families don't search to find things that make them come together as a family. Family members need to spend time on joint activities, or common projects; otherwise they lose the important sharing that helps maintain healthy and happy relationships. They lose the opportunity to connect with one another in ways that develop trust, respect, and love.

Reading together is an activity that families can make part of their daily routine. There's always time to read a page or two of a book, over breakfast in the morning or as part of a bedtime routine. Some families may choose to read a book at the same time as one another, all cuddled together on the couch with one person reading aloud to the others. In families with older children, parents may choose to read a book in advance, then talk together about it as children read through at their own pace.

The book you're holding here is an especially good choice for a family book, since it is engaging on many levels. Children in a range of ages will find a character that they can identify with, since the maturity of the characters range from naive, young Toddy to the wise Rufus. Adults may especially enjoy the care the author has taken to portray flora and fauna accurately throughout the book; providing a field guide to meadow living. Finally, interaction between parents and children is enhanced through the author's use of colorful vocabulary. Many terms in the book may be unfamiliar, especially to younger readers. The glossary provided can aid parents in explaining and exploring many new words in the book with children, creating a wonderful atmosphere for learning and sharing.

So, off you go! Catch up with Bunny Pufftail and Toddy, hop with them onto the frog ferry and the high wire skeedoodle, and join them in a world of exploration and amusement as you all head off on your autumn adventure.

Christina Yoshimura, Ph.D.
Professor, Department of Communication Studies
The University of Montana

Pufftail's Pointers for Parents

Dear Folks,

Bunnies believe that reading to our young ones is a very important part of their upbringing. It is a special time of cuddling and of sharing stories that can stir their imagination and spark their interest in learning. It sets a pattern for their life's journey.

We like to start when they are infants because reading while snuggling with your baby is a lovely combination. The first step in teaching them to read is to begin by pointing to the pictures as you read aloud. Use a dramatic voice or mimic the voice of an animal in the story. (Squeak like a mouse even!) Throw yourself into it! You will be making many happy memories.

As your young one becomes verbal, begin to use your finger (or in my case paw) to track the print as you read aloud. It will help to reinforce the idea that those squiggly things you're pointing to have meaning. With simple sentence picture books you can continue to point to the pictures and point to the word in the sentence that is shown in the picture. Example: The bunny went into the cabbage patch. Point to the word bunny and point to the picture of the bunny. Do the same with cabbage patch.

After they learn the alphabet and begin to identify sounds in words, start using easy reader books that they can read to you (even if they have memorized it). Ask them to find a particular word in the story. Then see how many times they can find that same word in the newspaper by coloring it in with a light colored crayon (I favor yellow and orange) Explain that it is alright to use a crayon to highlight words in a newspaper, but books are off limits!

Have a special place for books. Something at their eye level is always a plus. Teach proper care and use of their books. (Peanut butter and jelly sandwiches and books do not mix nor do nibbling radishes and carrots while reading.) Clean paws are important. Remember the old adage "Bunny see, Bunny do". If they see you set the example they will see the importance of doing it.

Give books as presents. If you don't know what book to give, locate someone who has a good background in quality children's books. A librarian, school teacher or bookstore clerk are some possibilities. First read the book yourself, if possible. If you like it, chances are your child will too. Plus you will be able to read it with more expression when you have read it yourself first.

Continue reading to your children as they grow older, and keep the drama going with that actor that lurks within you. When you come to a word that they don't know the meaning of, have them use the context of the sentence to get at its meaning. Have them tell you what they think it is. Look it up in the dictionary together. To reinforce the word, use it around the house. My father liked to use the word ensconced at the breakfast table. He would say "Would you please pass the carrots that you have ensconced on your side of the burrow?" Not only did it produce a laugh but also the word is permanently ensconced in my head!

Have a word of the day. Who can use it in a sentence the most times? Perhaps you can even use it as a game when you are on a long trip in the car. (Examples: Who can find a cupola on a house or barn? Who can find an equestrian or a pedestrian?)

Remember, words are the clothes that we wear (or in my case the fur that I wear). They give a lasting impression of how we wish to be seen by others. The words that are not so easily understood in this story are in italics and you will find a list of them along with their definitions at the end of the book.

My sincere wish for you is to have many happy memories reading this story as well as listening to your child read it back to you.

Your friend,
Bunny Pufftail

P.S. When reading this story aloud, say the **bold** typed words with emphasis. **HOP TO IT!**

Tails of
High Meadows

An Autumn Adventure

By Mary Stewart Granato

Illustrations by Sharon Pape

Chapter One

Greetings at High Meadow

Bunny Pufftail lived on a hill named High Meadow, a place so quiet that the wind spoke in breezy tones and a place so perfect that even the mosquitoes behaved themselves.

Bunny Pufftail was a young adult cottontail rabbit. Had she been born human, she would have been around twenty. She had soft brown fur and perky stand up ears which she always kept slightly bent. Not only did this fact make her a better listener, but it also gave her a cute appearance.

Usually Bunny Pufftail spent most of the day nibbling in among the tall, tender grasses of High Meadow, but on this particular day, she was standing in the *stubble* of new mown hay, looking far down into the valley below. Farmer

Ott, who owned the hill and surrounding fields, had mowed the day before.

It was the custom to mow the hill only once a year in response to his wife's request. She wanted the hill untouched until late summer so that the Meadow larks, Bobolinks and other grass nesting birds had a proper place to rear their young. In late July, the *fragrant* grasses were then gathered up into huge bales that resembled *mammoth* shredded wheat, dropped on the hill by some careless giant. Later on in the season, Farmer Ott would take the bales into his barn to be used during the long winter months as bedding for the cows.

High Meadow was also perfect in other ways. It was a perfect place for rabbits and it was a perfect place for the other animals that lived there as well. The rabbits spent the summer eating the tender shoots of alfalfa, oats, and barley and the mice found an endless supply of good seeds for summer eating and winter storing. The tall grasses also gave them good cover from the hawks that flew silently overhead.

The deer made several paths through High Meadow as they grazed their way up and across the hill. Sometimes all that you could see were the tops of their heads and from a distance; they looked like brown *periscopes*, floating in a sea of wavy green.

Foxes, coyotes, and even the occasional dog also criss-crossed High Meadow, looking for an unsuspecting rabbit, vole, or mouse. However, they had little success, as the meadow folk were usually a very alert bunch.

Bunny Pufftail squatted closely to one of the towering bales and remained there, hidden from any unseen enemies. She listened to the rusty gate call of the glossy black grackles, and the cheerful burbling of the bluebirds as they swooped and soared overhead.

As she hid there, she suddenly heard a squeak from within the bale. Bunny Pufftail pricked her ears toward the small sound and chuckled to herself.

"Toddy Mouse, you might as well show yourself. I'd know that squeak anywhere."

"Aw, shucks", replied Toddy, as she poked her tiny nose out from one of the several tunnels that zigzagged through the bale. This bale was actually a summer mouse hotel for all of Toddy's family, which consisted of her 16 brothers and sisters, plus over 100 cousins, uncles, aunts, including both sets of grandparents. Bunny Pufftail had tried counting them all once but had fallen asleep trying.

"How do you always know it's me?" queried the young mouse. I don't think I sound all **that** different from the rest of my family."

"I listen carefully. Although I do have excellent hearing, it's more important that I pay attention to every detail. For example, I can tell the difference between the way that you walk and the way that Rhonda walks. You even sneeze differently." (Rhonda was Toddy's twin sister. Usually, they were *inseparable*, but Mother Mouse had sent Rhonda off with an urgent delivery of thyme tea to their Great Aunt Lydia. Bunny Pufftail suspected that the real reason was to split the twins up for a while, as they had a tendency to get into mischief.)

Toddy popped out of the bale, brushed the seeds from her fur, and crouched by her rabbit friend. In mouse years she would have been *equivalent* to an eight year old human. She squinted into the sky as her eyes adjusted to the bright October sun. It was then that she noticed that Bunny Pufftail's eyes were fixed upon a certain field in the valley below. Toddy also noticed that the field was speckled with round orange things. She could see the stooping figure of Farmer Ott as he picked up one of these curious objects. She noticed that he waddled and staggered as he carried it to a huge crate stationed in the center of the field.

Toddy glanced up at Bunny Pufftail and asked, "What are those big roly-poly things anyway? Are they giant seeds? Is Farmer Ott going to eat them or do you suppose he'll store them for the winter? Do you think the meadow folk know if they're any good to eat? They sure are big. Why, I'll bet you could make a house out of one of those things. Well, at least a mouse could. It might be a bit small for you."

Bunny Pufftail waited until Toddy ran out of words and air and then replied. "I'm not exactly sure what they are, Toddy. Once when I was making my weekly carrot selection, I had a chance to make a close inspection. Thinking it might be some type of fat carrot, I bit into one. Not a bad taste, but definitely not carrot. I was thinking of going down there today to investigate further. Would you like to go with me for a closer look? You could ride on my back since it would be a pretty long walk for a mouse."

Toddy squeaked with delight, scampered up the side of the bale and tumbled back down, landing on a clump of hay which thankfully broke her fall. Bunny Pufftail gently picked her up and brushed her off.

"Before you start doing any more back flips, you need to ask for your mother's permission. She may have other things planned for you today."

Toddy quickly disappeared into the bale and Bunny Pufftail scoped out the safest route for them to take. A few minutes later Toddy again appeared, wearing a miniature straw hat.

"Momma said that I can go as long as I'm back before supper. Rhonda and I have to watch the babies while she cooks." Bunny Pufftail knew that this was no small task since there were six small babies to watch, and they all seemed to go off in different directions most of the time. Many times she had seen their Momma holding onto 6 little tails with one paw while she did her chores with the other.

Bunny Pufftail hunched down so that Toddy could climb on. Wiggling with delight, the mouse adjusted her hat and climbed aboard. Toddy gently held onto the fur of Bunny Pufftail's neck with both paws.

The rabbit had decided that the safest route to the valley below was to use the large hay bales as cover. As they started down the hill, she was careful to stay close to the shadowed side of the bale so that she could avoid the watchful eyes of any four legged *predators* (and any winged ones for that matter). As she zigged zagged down the hill from bale to bale, she stopped and froze every few moments hoping to draw less attention. Toddy tried to remain still in spite of her excitement. Momma had taught her at a very early age that unnecessary movement could be *fatal*, especially in an open field such as this.

The wind picked up as they made their way down the hill. A playful breeze surely would have blown off Toddy's hat, had it not been secured with a rubber band which Momma had thoughtfully fastened as a chin strap. Momma had also cut ear holes in the brim so that Toddy's ears could poke out and remain alert.

Finally the traveling *duo* reached the bottom of the hill. They had arrived at the edge of a deep wood on one side and an open field on the other. Beyond this field lay Peeper

Pond. Bunny Pufftail began to hop slowly through this open space.

"Why are we going this way toward Peeper Pond?" asked Toddy. "I thought you'd take the forest route to get to Farmer Ott's field."

"The Woods are especially dangerous this time of year, Toddy," replied Bunny Pufftail. "The foxes and coyotes are there now training their young ones to hunt. I'd rather take my chances through Peeper Pond than end up being chased by a bunch of yapping pups and possibly get eaten as well. Besides, it's a shorter route to the farmer's field this way."

Toddy was just about to ask how Bunny Pufftail intended to get across the pond, but before she got the words out of her mouth, Bunny Pufftail said, "Hang on tightly, I'm going to speed up a bit."

And with a blur of brown fur Bunny Pufftail *hastened* toward the swamp known as Peeper Pond.

Chapter Two
Peeper Pond

Bunny Pufftail tore through the open field so fast that Toddy was being bounced and thrown in every direction. Her hat slid down over her eyes, blocking her view. Desperately she clung to Bunny Pufftail's fur and finally was able to paw her way up to one of her ears where she grabbed with her front paws and hung on. Looming high above them on both sides lay a forest of cattails. A young box turtle narrowly missed being stepped on by Bunny Pufftail when she finally came to a halt under a large willow tree that hung out over the pond.

Immediately the waters edge exploded into a leaping mass of frogs that had been sunning themselves on the shore. One minute the water was churning with escaping legs of liquid green and the next moment, the pond was still. The only evidence that proved the frogs had been there at all was a series of waves that came rippling out in circles from the center of the pond.

The first to pop his head up and to see what had caused all the commotion was an enormous bullfrog. What he saw was a very surprised mouse in a cockeyed straw hat sitting atop a rabbit, a rabbit that he instantly recognized.

"Pufftail, old friend," laughed the bullfrog. "It's good to see you on this sparkling October day."

The other frogs began surfacing once they sensed that there was no danger and gathered round their bullfrog leader.

"Jerome," chuckled a breathless Bunny Pufftail. "Where have you been? Hiding under a lily pad?"

"Actually you're not far off. I've been checking out several nice mud beds in the pond. Fall will soon be upon us, and as you know, we will need to bury ourselves for the coming winter. There's nothing like a good bed of soft mud to snooze in while the cold winds blow."

The large frog hopped out of the water and plopped himself down next to the rabbit and mouse.

"What brings you here, my fine furry friend? And by the way, who's the little one in the hat?"

"Oh, I forgot that you two hadn't met before. Please allow me to introduce Toddy Fieldmouse, daughter of Esther and Fred. Toddy, this is Jerome Bullfrog, the leader of Peeper Pond."

Jerome bent at the waist and bowed as best he could, considering his bulgy middle. He extended his long knobby fingers to Toddy. Shyly, and with some trepidation, she took his hand in her paw. Expecting it to be wet and slimy, Toddy was surprised that his hand was almost dry.

"I guess he must dry out pretty fast when he's out of the water for very long," she thought.

Bunny Pufftail turned toward Jerome and said, "We are headed over to Farmer Ott's field to investigate the orange things that he planted there. I thought it might be a good idea to take the shortcut through Peeper Pond. Besides, Toddy has never been on the frog ferry before, and since it won't be running much more this season, I thought that this might be a good day for it."

Toddy gave her rabbit friend a puzzled look. "Frog ferry? What's that?"

A smile began to stretch across Jerome's wide mouth. The frog ferry was his creation and over the years it had become one of the main attractions of Peeper Pond. All the local mice, chipmunks, squirrels and other dry land creatures used the ferry as a means to shorten their trip to the farmer's field during the growing season. Very often, piles of corn on the cob, beans, peas, carrots, and other vegetables could be seen being hoisted onto the ferry by a group of very powerful looking chipmunks know as the Rowdy Rodents. All through the growing season, they hauled the fresh produce onto the ferry. The frogs would then push it across the pond where it would be unloaded by the Rowdies (as they were called by the locals), and divided up by the animals to be shared equally. The raccoons and crows were banned from the ferry as they had a reputation for taking more food than they needed. Once, these rascals had tried to overload the ferry with their hoard and had managed to sink it. It took Jerome and the other frogs two days to get the ferry unstuck from the muddy bottom and clean up the mess.

Jerome hopped closer to Bunny Pufftail and said, "It would be my pleasure to take you both across the pond on the ferry. You happened to catch our last ferry run for this year. I only wish I could join you on the rest of your adventure. But on these legs I don't think I'd make it back before winter set in. I've always wondered about those orange things though. Don't know of anyone besides Farmer Ott who grows 'em. Don't look very edible, at least ways not to our folk."

With that, Jerome swelled up his throat and emitted a loud "KNEE DEEP!" Immediately, eight bullfrogs, almost as big as Jerome, splashed into the pond from the opposite shore, where the grasses and cattails grew especially thick. As the frogs began to swim, a portion of the shoreline broke away from the rest and the frogs positioned themselves around it. From a distance, it looked like a tiny floating island covered with tufts, cattails, and other varieties of water plants. In truth it was the frog ferry. Protruding from both sides of this cleverly camouflaged craft were six Popsicle sticks (three to a side). It was to each Popsicle stick that each frog stationed himself. Grasping the stick with their front legs, the frogs pushed off with their powerful hind legs. In a few minutes they reached the shore where Toddy and Bunny Pufftail stood. By furiously backpedaling, the frogs were able to slow the ferry down enough for a safe docking. It slid smoothly into a niche in the shoreline and once again it blended in with the surrounding leafage.

Jerome pulled his massive body up to the stern of the boat and plopped himself down on a mammoth toadstool. Since Jerome was sensitive about his family heritage, all the members of the community referred to this giant mushroom as Jerome's throne. From his position in the back of the boat atop his "throne" the bullfrog had a clear view of the route that they would take ahead.

By using the protruding grasses as ropes, Bunny Pufftail and Toddy made their way up the side of the ferry until they found a little recessed spot covered in moss. Here they nestled themselves in for the ride. A gentle breeze began blowing, just enough to ruffle their warm fur.

All at once Jerome belched out a loud "CROAK!"

"Frogs at the ready!" he bellowed. "Frogs set! Frogs go! Stroke —— Croak —— Stroke —— Croak!" The call went out over the pond and echoed back to them. Keeping rhythm with this call, the six frogs began kicking their powerful back legs in steady strokes.

A few minutes later, the frog ferry arrived at another niche on the far shore near the apple orchard. It slowed and glided into the surrounding cattails and grasses, and once again became part of the natural scene.

Bunny Pufftail and Toddy climbed paw over paw down the side of the ferry, being very careful not to step on any frog's heads as they made their way down to the water's edge. Here, Toddy climbed up to Bunny Pufftail's neck, thus avoiding a soggy walk to shore. Bunny Pufftail then sloshed her way along the bank and up to dry ground. She looked back towards Jerome who was still seated in back of the boat.

"How much do we owe you, Jerome?"

The frog just laughed. "Usually, the going price for rabbits is a jug of clover wine, but since I know that it's not in season, you can pay me in the spring. Your reputation for being a rabbit of high integrity and good moral standing is widely known. Since this is the last run of the ferry this season, I probably won't see you until next spring. I trust you'll take the wood's way back?" Bunny Pufftail nodded yes.

"Have a safe and happy trip. I'll see you on the other side of winter. Bye-bye, Toddy Fieldmouse."

The two adventurers waved their paws, thanked their host, and headed up the bank toward the apple grove.

Chapter Three
Rufus

Bunny Pufftail, with Toddy sitting between her ears, *loped* up the well worn path to the apple grove. The *fragrance* of apples was sweet upon the air and made Toddy's nose twitch and her mouth water. The round, ripe fruit hung suspended from the low branches and every now and then the quiet scene was shaken by a loud 'thump,' as an apple broke loose and bounced to the ground. Bunny Pufftail had to keep one eye on the path and one eye above, in hopes that they might avoid being bonked on the head by falling fruit.

As the two *emerged* from the apple grove, Bunny Pufftail hopped off the path and crawled under a clump of ferns. Toddy had to duck down and grasp onto both of the rabbit's ears to avoid being brushed off. The mouse began to imagine that she was riding an elephant deep within an *exotic* jungle.

As Bunny Pufftail squatted there, her sharp ears picked up the sound of a familiar voice; a human voice.

"Plumy?" Bunny Pufftail wondered aloud.

"What are you talking about? What's a Plumy?" *inquired* Toddy as she stood between the rabbit's ears.

"She is a human child that I met last spring. Her full name is Pluma Rachel Ott, Plumy for short. She's the only child of Farmer Ott, what humans call a six and a half year old. She was out in her backyard and I was nibbling some tender young dandelions by their house. You'll never guess what she was doing," whispered Bunny Pufftail.

"What?" whispered Toddy, all wiggly with curiosity.

"She was picking eggs. Not regular eggs mind you. Eggs that looked as if a rainbow fell on them. They must have been laid by some pretty wild chickens.

"Oh my goodness!" whispered Toddy. "What happened?"

"She kept picking eggs out of all sorts of odd places, from under the porch, the laundry basket and even the mailbox. Very strange."

"You're kidding!" exclaimed Toddy.

"No, rabbit's honor," replied Bunny Pufftail. "And that's not the strangest part either. When she finally saw me hiding under the tulips she said, 'Hello there, Easter Bunny. Thank you for the eggs.'"

"Jeepers!" exclaimed Toddy.

"Then she told me her name and said that she would leave me a carrot by the porch as a thank you gift."

"Did she?" questioned Toddy.

"A most delicious one. I ended up eating half of it there and taking the rest home with me. I hope that this Easter Bunny person didn't mind me eating his treat. I left a message for him with the local blue jays stating that he was most welcome to stop by my burrow anytime for a substitute carrot. He hasn't shown up yet though. Perhaps he's too busy with all those eggs."

"I guess," replied Toddy, wide-eyed.

Bunny Pufftail crept closer to the place from which the sound had come. Pluma Rachel Ott was sitting in the field, perched on one of the large orange things. Next to her sat her big black and white dog, Rufus, and, hooked under his collar, was Sally Ann, Plumy's rag doll.

Rufus gave Plumy a questioning look, but continued to sit *obediently*.

"Now Sally Ann, I know you've never been horseback riding before, so it's very important that you hang on tightly. Rufus is a very sure footed *steed*." (Her mother had read the word the night before in a bedtime story, so Plumy tried it out at every opportunity.)

"He's never thrown anyone, but nevertheless, you must be careful not to startle him. So no yelling or poking him in the ribs, okay?"

The rag doll looked back with blank button eyes and a stitched on smile, while Rufus rolled his old brown eyes in response. He became more and more restless and finally he shook himself the way he always did after a good swim. No luck. Sally Ann stuck. Plumy gently took Rufus' face into her hands and spoke softly.

"That wasn't very nice of you, Rufus. She could have been hurt. You **know** better."

Rufus' tail drooped. His head hung down. Plumy put her arms around his neck and hugged his warm black fur. Once again his tail was a happy wag.

"I'm sorry if I hurt your feelings, Rufus. I know you didn't mean to scare Sally Ann. Try to be more careful, okay?"

Rufus' tail continued to wag. Suddenly his big leathery nose caught the scent of Bunny Pufftail and Toddy. Before he could bark, Bunny Pufftail shot out from her hiding place and headed straight for the center of the field towards a huge crate of the orange things. Toddy squatted down between Bunny Pufftail's ears and clung like a rider on a race horse. While they crisscrossed through the field, Rufus set out at his fastest pace, leaving Plumy alone in the field. The best that he could do was a slow trot. Like an oversized pin-wheel, his whip of a tail went round and round, *propelling* him forward and giving him added *thrust*.

Plumy stood and watched as Rufus continued to chase after the departing duo.

"Rufus come back here, now!" she called. He turned and looked at her for only a moment.

"A dog has to do what a dog has to do," his eyes and bark told her. "*Trespassers* in the master's field are not allowed." He turned and ran toward the crate where he had seen the rabbit go continuing in hot *pursuit*.

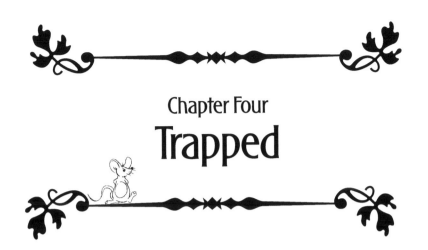

Chapter Four
Trapped

When Bunny Pufftail finally reached the crate, she managed to squeeze in between two broken slats. There she crawled in and wedged herself under a mammoth orange thing. Toddy scampered down from Bunny Pufftail and before long; Rufus came panting up the field.

"You there, in the crate. *Stowaways* are not allowed. Those pumpkins belong to the master."

Bunny Pufftail thought to herself "So **that's** what they are," and peeked out from under the "pumpkin" to get a better look. For all of his gruffness, she could see that the dog was reasonable and fair-minded. She saw no bristly tail nor snarly teeth, a sure sign of trouble for a rabbit. She also noticed that he spoke with *authority* but wasn't rude. In her young bunny life, she had *encountered* a variety of dogs. She knew when to run and when to offer politeness. As the rabbits of High Meadow would say, "This dog is more bark than bite – more wag than woof." And furthermore, Bunny Pufftail recognized the doll hanging from under his neck as belonging to the Ott's daughter. She was certain that the parents would never put their daughter in harm's way by allowing her to play with a fierce dog. She inched closer to the slats to where Rufus stood, until dog and rabbit were almost nose to nose. Rufus waited. (If truth be told, he was too tired to do otherwise.)

Bunny Pufftail spoke softly. "Sir, it was not our intention to trespass. I've come seeking information about the orange things growing in the field. I brought my friend Toddy with me to share in this adventure."

Toddy peeked out from behind her friend, her curiosity *conquering* her fear. Rufus eyed the mouse, but said nothing.

He had learned that speaking did not always help thinking, and right now he needed time to think.

Toddy's curiosity finally overpowered her fear of the old dog, and she crept from her hiding place. After poking her head through the slats to get a better look at Rufus, the mouse instantly *regretted* it.

The wide brim of her straw hat became stuck like a cork in a bottle. Had she thought about it, she could have easily pulled the rubber band chin strap off and freed herself. However, panic and fear began to rise in her, choking out all calm and reasonable thought. She began to twist and tug at the hat and her breathing came in short little squeaking gasps. Before Bunny Pufftail could step forward, Rufus took the matter into his own hands (Or into his paws, actually). He shoved his nose between the slats just above Toddy's head and rammed his big snout forward like a wedge. The aged wooden slats snapped and splintered, popping Toddy free. She fell backwards and sat down, hard. Her nose stung from the snap of the rubber band strap and she rubbed her tender bottom.

When she finally looked up, she saw Bunny Pufftail standing over her, and, looming high above them both, was Rufus. He stared back at them and then spoke.

"Are you all right, Mousie?"

Toddy's mouth dropped open. She sat back wide-eyed, gaping up at the *gargantuan* dog.

"You, you…can talk!" she finally sputtered. "I didn't know dogs could talk."

"All dogs can talk," said Bunny Pufftail. "What is unusual is that this one speaks the language of High Meadow."

"We apologize for causing any trouble for you, sir," said Bunny Pufftail, turning her head up toward the dog.

"We came to investigate the orange things, what you called pumpkins, I believe? We mean no harm. As soon as I'm sure that Toddy is okay, we will be on our way. Thank you for what you did for her."

This time it was Rufus whose mouth dropped open. For what he saw was so strange, he could only stare. Toddy mouse had picked herself up off the floor, stepped forward and shyly extended her paw toward him.

"My name is Toddy. What's yours? Thank you for rescuing me," said Toddy bashfully.

Suddenly she realized how silly it was for her to try and shake a paw that was bigger than she was. How foolish she must look!

Rufus seemed to realize what she was thinking, for he extended his paw through the slats to where the mouse stood.

"My name is Rufus. Glad to make your acquaintance."

Toddy reached up and touched his big paw. How soft and warm it felt! Before the big dog could protest, she *clambered* up on top of his paw and sat down. Rufus looked down at Toddy sitting on his foot. He looked over at Bunny

Pufftail and rolled his eyeballs. "Does she do this with every strange dog she meets?" he inquired.

Bunny Pufftail laughed. "No, you're the first. She's never met a real dog before. Of course she's seen pictures of them at school, but it's not quite the same thing, is it? By the way, my name is Bunny Pufftail."

"I apologize for being so cross with you before," said Rufus. "Someone has been coming into the field and smashing the master's pumpkins. I realize now that it couldn't be you. I guess I didn't think things through before I reacted."

"Well, why don't we just start over?" said Bunny Pufftail. "Toddy, you need to get off Rufus' foot."

"Good idea," replied Rufus. "I wouldn't want to step on you by accident."

Toddy quickly got off and smiled up at him.

After proper *introductions* were made, Rufus spoke. "You said that you came to learn about pumpkins."

"Yes," said Bunny Pufftail. "Just what are they, exactly?"

Looking around for a soft place to sit, Rufus eyed a patch of grass and sat down with his paws outstretched. Toddy immediately took this as an invitation and scurried forth. She stopped just short of his paws and asked in her most polite voice, "May I please sit on your paw? It's so warm and toasty."

Bunny Pufftail was about to object when Rufus chuckled. "Climb on up, little Toddy. Never knew mice liked to sit on dogs before."

"They don't," replied Bunny Pufftail. "Toddy doesn't know enough to be afraid. It really drove her mother to distraction when she was a baby. She even had to be rescued from a cat once. But that's another story. Let's get back to the topic of pumpkins. What can you tell us about them?"

"Well," said Rufus. "Pumpkins are a kind of food that people like to eat in the fall, mostly perhaps because it takes them that long to ripen. Mrs. Ott likes to cook them up and put them in a thing she calls a pie. She often leaves them on the kitchen window sill to cool. It's a heavenly scent, I can assure you. Only my loyalty to my mistress prevents me from eating it.

"There is another thing that humans do with pumpkins, although personally I can't see how it makes a whole lot of sense."

"What's that?" inquired Toddy and Bunny Pufftail at the same time.

"Well, around this time of year, the family selects a large pumpkin, cuts a whole in the top, digs out the seeds, and then wonder of wonders, carves a scary face on one side."

"Really?" asked Toddy, *awestruck*.

"That's not all," said Rufus, *confident* that he had the full attention of his audience.

"They put a lit candle inside it and put it out on the porch at night. Then they wait for Halloween."

"Who's that?" asked Toddy.

"It's a what, not a who," said Rufus. "It's a day when young children go from house to house, dressed in strange clothes and beg for food."

"What kind of food?" said Toddy hungrily.

"Food that Mrs. Ott says will spoil your appetite."

"What's an appetite?" inquired Toddy, whose stomach was now making little growly noises.

"I believe it is a place in a young one's stomach where anything that has sugar in it is not allowed until fresh fruit and vegetables have been eaten. At least this is what Plumy has led me to believe. Mrs. Ott keeps a close eye on her daughter's, that I can tell you. Speaking of Plumy, here she comes!"

Before Toddy and Bunny Pufftail could hide, Plumy came running up, breathless from her run across the field.

She looked from the mouse to the rabbit. Suddenly her eyes widened with *recognition*.

"Rufus, I didn't know you knew the Easter Bunny!

Shouldn't he be home painting eggs? Why is there a mouse sitting on your foot?"

"What did she say?" asked Toddy, looking up at the dog.

"She wants to know who you are and why I'm not painting Easter eggs," said Bunny Pufftail before Rufus could answer.

"Lordy Lou, you understand kidese!" said Rufus.

"Learned it at Bunny school. I took two years of kidese, plus three years of dog *dialects*. Thought it might be useful some day. I guess I was right."

"You certainly are full of surprises," said Rufus. "Next thing you know you'll be telling me you know how to water-ski."

"Well, I don't know about that, but I certainly have the feet for it, don't you think?" laughed Bunny Pufftail. "Right now I think you need to talk with your Plumy. I have a feeling she could help us out with the pumpkin issue."

"Quite right," exclaimed Rufus, gently tipping Toddy off onto the ground. He got up stiffly, stretched his legs, and walked directly in front of Plumy. With the rag doll still dangling from his collar, Rufus sat down and put his paw out. Plumy, recognizing the signal squatted down in front of him. Holding his paw in her hands, she placed it over her heart. Rufus looked straight into her eyes. His breathing slowed. Plumy *concentrated*, her eyes fixed on Rufus only.

"What's happening?" whispered Toddy.

"They're communicating," replied Bunny Pufftail. "Some people talk to their dogs and the dogs understand. Some dogs talk to people and the people understand. Plumy must be a very special person. Her dog talks to her and she understands him. Sometimes they don't even need words."

"But how can that be?" replied Toddy.

"I guess they trust and love each other a lot."

At that moment, the distant chugging of Mr. Ott's tractor could be heard as it started across the field toward them.

Rufus and Plumy ended their conversation, got up, and joined the others.

"I explained to Plumy about who you are, and for that matter, who you aren't," said Rufus to Bunny Pufftail. "She has a terrific idea. If you two hide in the pumpkin crate, you could get a free ride to the farmhouse. She says that she and her mom are carving the pumpkin today, and that you could watch. They do it outside by the bird sanctuary so that the birds can have the seeds."

As Rufus spoke to two travelers, Plumy kept her eyes on the ever *advancing* tractor.

"Quick," said Plumy. "Hide in the crate before my Daddy sees you."

The two stowaways scrambled back into the crate and managed to squeeze into a corner where a mammoth pumpkin could not fit.

Mr. Ott drove the tractor around to the side of the crate and stopped. Attached to the front of the tractor was a fork-lift which he used to hoist the pumpkin *laden* crate into the air. He called down to Plumy who was untying Sally Ann from Rufus' collar.

"I see you found Sally Ann's horse," he muttered. "Been giving her another riding lesson?"

Plumy clutched her beloved doll and climbed up by her father. She smiled up at her dad, but did not respond to his teasing. Her mind was on secret guests and pumpkins.

Rufus kept well away from the tractor activity as the heavy crate was lifted into air. The smell and noise of the machine made his fur stand on end.

He put his tail into whirling motion and began to follow from a safe distance as the tractor crept slowly across the field.

The smell of dried grass and diesel fumes filled Plumy's nose and the loud chugging filled her ears. When the tractor finally reached the end of the plowed field to where the old farm road began, Mr. Ott shifted gears and the tractor lurched forward. As they sped along the dirt road, the wind whipped Plumy's hair back from her face. Her cheeks became rosy with the coolness of the autumn day. With one arm on the steering wheel and one arm wrapped firmly around his daughter, Mr. Ott steered the tractor, the pumpkins and the two stowaways through the trees that lined both sides of the old farm road. Plumy felt safe and cozy as she snuggled closer to her dad. She wore the *serene* smile of one who has a pleasant secret.

Chapter Five
The Farm

The signal of oncoming fall was everywhere. The squirrels *frantically* scampered from tree to tree, looking for one more nut to store. Blackbirds and starlings flocked and swooped, telling their members that it would soon be time to fly to warmer places. Even the occasional leaf seemed to sense the change and would release its grasp from a branch, only to be caught on the wind and spiral out of control.

Bunny Pufftail and Toddy were having a dreadful time in the pumpkin crate. Their stomachs were in knots from being thrown from side to side as the tractor bumped its way along an endless collection of ruts and rocky *outcroppings*. Toddy clutched Bunny Pufftail's front leg with all four paws.

She vowed that if she made it out of this *ordeal* alive, she'd never ever go near another stinking tractor as long as she lived.

Bunny Pufftail was feeling extremely *squeamish*, but put on her brave face, since she thought it would only make Toddy feel worse to know that she was afraid as well. Thank goodness the pumpkins were jammed in so tightly, for otherwise they would have been squashed flat! Suddenly the barn came into view and the tractor *lurched* to a stop by the barn doors. The fork lift lowered the crate to the ground with a bump, and the tractor backed up. Plumy got down with her doll as Mr. Ott drove the tractor inside the barn.

Immediately the stowaways made their get-away. Toddy climbed aboard Bunny Pufftail once again and they made a dash for what seemed to be a miniature house stationed right next to the barn. "Could this be a house for elves?" wondered Toddy. As they drew closer, the smell of Rufus was everywhere. Realizing that they had stumbled onto his home, they crept inside and waited. Plumy had watched their escape and casually walked toward the doghouse. She laid Sally Ann on the roof to keep her out of the dirt.

Just then a woman came out onto the porch of the house. A red checked apron covered her faded denim skirt and white blouse. Her hands were gloved in flour and there was even a smudge of white on her nose. To Bunny Pufftail she looked like a tall version of Plumy.

"Time to wash up, you two. Lunch is in ten minutes. I've got a nice loaf of warm bread that I just took out of the oven. Any takers?"

"Race you to the house, Daddy," Plumy called as she started running toward the house.

"Whoa there, horsie," her father called. "Aren't you forgetting something?"

Plumy stopped, turned and walked toward her father with a questioning look on her face.

"There's a certain hungry dog coming up the lane that

needs lunch, too. Old Rufus'll think that you don't love him anymore."

"Sorry, Daddy, I forgot. Tell Mommy I'll be in as quickly as I can."

"Ok, Sport. Make sure that you put the lid back on tightly to the dog food can. Don't want any critters getting a free lunch."

"Alright," she called, as she walked slowly to the barn.

Plumy entered through the big doors that led to the basement floor where the tractor was parked. The air was damp and musty there, unlike the floor above, where the bales of fragrant hay were stored. Plumy disliked the basement and moved quickly to finish her chores and get out. There were too many dark corners and old cobwebs in here as far as she was concerned. She wrinkled her nose as she breathed in the stale air. Quickly, she walked to a large metal can that stored the dog food, removed the lid, and dug out a large scoop of dried food with a coffee can that was kept there. She carefully replaced the lid, turned and walked quickly back toward the big doors, where the fresh air and daylight awaited. Standing in the doorway was Rufus, wagging his tail politely. As she approached him, the creepy feelings melted away and she shivered with relief. Rufus knew how she felt about the basement, and *accompanied* her there whenever he could. Plumy squatted down by the old dog and hugged his head in her lap.

"After we both have lunch, I'll meet you in the bird *sanctuary*. Make sure no one sees our friends. Mommy might think Bunny Pufftail is here to eat her flowers. And I don't think she likes mice, even if they are wearing hats. By the way, where do you suppose she got it? It looks like the one Sally Ann had last spring. But never mind that right now. You'll need to *escort* them to the sanctuary. I saw them duck into your house a little while ago."

Plumy got up and the two walked towards the doghouse. After pouring the food into his dish and checking to see whether he had enough water, she placed the coffee can on the grass.

"We'll return the coffee can later, ok? Right now I've got to go eat." With that, she plucked Sally Ann off of the doghouse roof and walked towards Rufus.

Glancing towards the doghouse, Plumy said," Perhaps your friends would like to join you for lunch." She patted the dog's head. "Bye-bye for now. See you later in the sanctuary." With that she skipped off towards the house, hugging her hatless doll.

"Did you hear what she said about my hat?" questioned Toddy. "I feel awful now. What should I do?" asked Toddy *plaintively*.

"We will make sure that she gets her hat back before we leave here today." said Bunny Pufftail. "No need to feel bad Toddy. It wasn't your fault. It's my responsibility. I guess I should have made more *inquiries* than I did, but don't worry. We'll take care that she gets it. I'm sure that Rufus can *intercede* for us and explain the situation. Right now we need food. I always think better on a full stomach, don't you?" asked Bunny Pufftail.

"Yes indeed," said Toddy. "My tummy has been talking for the last half hour."

The mouse and rabbit crept toward the doorway and peered out. They looked both ways and only then stepped into the sunshine. Although they trusted Rufus completely now and were pretty sure of Plumy, they were still in *foreign* territory. One could never be too careful. Toddy eyed the dog dish and once again her stomach growled, this time loud enough for all of them to hear.

"Rufus, after you eat, could we go straight to the bird-feeder?" Bunny Pufftail asked. "Someone's stomach is a bit empty. And may we have a drink from your water dish?

"Of course. You're welcome to try some of my food too."

"Thank you for your *hospitality*, Rufus. You're a true

gentleman," said Bunny Pufftail.

The two guests walked over to the water dish. Bunny Pufftail had no difficulty in obtaining a nice long drink, but for Toddy it was a long stretch. She had to stand on her toes and even then, only her paws reached the water. She splashed some towards her face, only succeeding in getting her whiskers wet. Finally she leaned over so far that she fell in, hat and all. Rufus quickly stuck his paw in the dish. Toddy scrambled up his foot, and jumped down to the grass. Immediately she began to lick the water off her fur.

"Well, I finally got a drink," said Toddy, laughing.

"Looks like you got a bath as well," chuckled Rufus.

Having *quenched* her thirst, Bunny Pufftail decided to give the dog food a try. Although the crunchiness was appealing, the taste and smell were *appalling*.

She wrinkled her nose and sneezed.

"Bless you," said Rufus and Toddy in *unison*.

Rufus gave her a sideways glance, and sensing her displeasure, decided it was time to move on to more suitable food. With the dog leading the way, the *trio* headed up the path toward the house. By walking near to the bushes that grew along the porch, Rufus was able to give his new friends a sheltered path on which to walk. When they reached the back of the house, Rufus stopped and looked both ways. Spread out before them was a vast lawn that sloped downward to a small wooded area. A stone path cut through this lawn, ending at the trees. *Concealed* in these little woods was a bird sanctuary, complete with several feeders, a rock pool, nesting boxes, and even a gazebo for human visitors. It was to this place that Rufus now proceeded. Toddy climbed up onto Bunny Pufftail's back once again, for it was essential that they get across the open field quickly. Wide open spaces were extremely dangerous for mice and rabbits. A hawk *hovering* a thousand feet above could spot a small animal, swoop down and be gone with it in a matter of seconds. Of course, with Rufus as their escort, they had less to fear.

However, Bunny Pufftail took her responsibility of protecting Toddy very seriously.

The threesome finally made it to the end of the lawn and entered the woods. A large cocky blue jay gave a warning call. Immediately all the birds scattered to the trees above and scolded as they flew.

Chapter Six
The Sanctuary

Rufus stopped beneath the tree of the perching blue jay and looked up.

"Jay Jay, it's me, Rufus. And I've brought some guests."

Jacob Jerry Blue Jay, Jay Jay to his friends, flew down from the treetop and made a bounced landing on a low branch. He continued to bob up and down until the branch came to a stop. Cocking his head to one side, the *saucy* bird looked at the threesome.

"Rufus! Dog among dogs! As I live and breathe! Is that you? I haven't seen you since Auntie Caw Caw's sunflower seed fest! Has that Plumy girl been keepin' you busy? Still got you playin' horsie? Speaking of horsie, why's 'at mouse riding that bunny?"

Jay Jay reminded Rufus of a plastic, wind up duck that Plumy had. It quacked continuously until its spring unwound. When he was certain that Jay Jay had "run down," Rufus spoke.

"Jay Jay, I'd like you to meet Bunny Pufftail and Toddy Fieldmouse, some folks from High Meadow. Bunny Pufftail, Toddy, this is Jacob Jerry Blue Jay, guardian of the bird sanctuary and seed eater *extraordinaire*."

Jay Jay made a low bow towards the newcomers, fanning the crest on his head as is the custom of well mannered blue jays.

"Nice ta meetcha, nice ta meetcha," he said. He flew down and landed on Rufus' back so as to get a better look at the shorter visitors. Blue jays, like their cousins the crows, are an inquisitive lot. Rufus often complimented Jay Jay in front of other birds by referring to him as a "crow in blue clothes." This was high praise indeed, for like his crow cousins, he was cautious, watchful, and smart. And like his crow cousins, he also had a big mouth. It came in handy when warning everyone of *imminent* danger. It also came in handy for consuming twenty to thirty seeds in one gulp.

Jay Jay suddenly cocked his head and spoke, "'Scuse me a second." Pointing his beak towards the birds that remained hidden in the trees, Jay Jay planted his feet and tail firmly into Rufus' back and squawked.

The coast is clear!

No danger is near!

So have no fear

Cause Jay Jay is here!"

The birds began to flutter their way back toward the sanctuary feeders, calling as they flew.

"Thanks Jay Jay!"

"Appreciate it, Jay Jay."

"Good job, Jay Jay!"

Toddy's mouth dropped open and Bunny Pufftail

gaped at the *spectacle*. Rufus just stood there with an amused expression and waited for Jay Jay to hop off. The bird seemed in no hurry and was enjoying the reaction of Toddy and Bunny Pufftail.

The blue jay turned towards them and spoke in a *dramatic* whisper.

"I like to give them all 'a bit of the rhyme,' as my dear uncle Caw Caw used to say. So much more interestin' that just plain old 'All is secure!'"

At this point Jay Jay began to stare intently at Toddy. Suddenly he grinned all the way back to where Toddy thought that his ears might be.

"How silly of me not to have recognized it before!" exclaimed Jay Jay to Toddy.

"I think I answered my own question 'bout why you're ridin' 'nstead of walkin'. You don't want to end up as a tasty morsel for some hawk, do ya?"

Toddy managed a weak smile and gulped.

"I think we need to continue on to the sanctuary," said Rufus. "We need to feed our guests before Plumy and her mother arrive."

Jay Jay leaped off of Rufus, flew over to a stone wall that marked the entrance to the bird sanctuary and bounced as he landed.

"Why goodness me, why didn't you say so in the first place? Here I am jabberin' away about hawks and the like and we've got big time company comin'! Rufus, you know how I feel about Plumy and her mom! Most humans don't like blue jays much. They think we're too loud and too sassy. Those Ott gals think I'm a real cutie. Why, many's the time when I've entertained 'em with my seed eatin' abilities."

Jay Jay was so engrossed in his one sided conversation, that he hardly noticed that the trio had continued on ahead of him and had entered the sanctuary. He launched himself off the stone wall and flew over the guests, continuing his chatter.

"Right this way! Right this way! Comin' through! Comin' through!" he called. The feeding stations became a colorful blur of feathers as most of the birds beat a hasty retreat to the trees once more.

The chickadees and titmice, being of a braver nature, were the only birds that remained. Toddy leaned over and whispered softly into Bunny Pufftail's ear.

"Does Jay Jay **ever** stop talking?"

"Well, he certainly seems to be a loquacious bird, doesn't he?" replied Bunny Pufftail.

"If that means he talks a lot, then I totally agree!" giggled Toddy.

"You'll find the feeding trays straight ahead," said Rufus to Bunny Pufftail. "After you deposit Toddy under that big one in the center, I'll show you where there is some nice tender grass for your lunch."

"I'm not so certain I should leave Toddy for that long," replied Bunny Pufftail. "All kinds of things could happen and she is my responsibility."

Jay Jay, overhearing the conversation, blurted out, "Why, not to worry, not to worry. I'll stand guard while you get a bite to eat!"

"Thank you for your offer, but I wouldn't want to impose on you," said Bunny Pufftail. (If truth be told, she wasn't too sure of Jay Jay's *dependability*.)

Rufus interceded at this point. "The sanctuary is 95% cat, snake, and hawk proof. It won't be just Jay Jay on watch. All the birds pitch in to warn the others. I dare say Toddy will be left in capable hands, or claws rather. Besides, you won't be gone that long or that far. It's just a little down the path near the gazebo. Toddy needs to learn to fend for herself a little bit, don't you think? What better place to practice *independence* than in the sanctuary?"

Bunny Pufftail considered these arguments thoughtfully, and although she had some *apprehension* about it, she finally consented. She trusted Rufus' judgement and after all, she would only be a hop away, would she not?

After depositing Toddy beneath the biggest of the seed platforms and giving last minute instructions in mouse safety, Bunny Pufftail hopped off with Rufus towards a *veritable* salad bar of tender grasses.

Chapter Seven
The Platform

Toddy watched them go for a minute or two, and then got down to the business of eating. She began poking through the pebbles and grass, occasionally discovering a lost bit of cracked corn or sunflower seed that had dropped from the platform above. She even discovered a plump raisin, but then thought better of eating it, for it appeared to be walking! Upon close examination, she found a couple of tough-looking ants underneath that were attempting to haul it away. Tug-of-war over food never seemed like a good idea.

"Hello down there!" called a voice from above.

Toddy tipped her head way back and looked up. Two small, bright eyed birds peered over the edge of the seed platform. She recognized one as a black-capped chickadee, but the other bird was unknown to her. Although it was about the same size as the chickadee, it was grayish in color with a white underbelly and had a crest on its head similar to Jay Jay's.

"Come on up," said the chickadee. "It's more pleasant dining up here with us than *foraging* alone down there among the weeds."

"How do I go about getting up there?" inquired Toddy nervously.

"Just climb the maple tree. The bark is rough, so it should be an easy climb. At least that's what the other mice tell us. When you get underneath the seed platform, you'll find a well worn knot-hole that will bring you right up through to the top. You won't see the hole until you're almost on top of it, because it's hidden by a bump in the tree. The garden wall mice use it all the time. Matter of fact, there's a mouse up here right now."

Once again Toddy's curiosity overcame her fear. Besides, she was so hungry, she was even *contemplating* a raisin battle with the ants.

Toddy easily climbed the maple tree and went up and over the bump, which turned out to be part of a tree limb that had not been cut off completely. Poking whiskers and face through the hole first, Toddy saw a veritable feast before her. Mounds of seeds stretched out in every direction. The chickadee hopped over and extended her beak toward Toddy.

"Grab onto my beak and I'll pull you the rest of the way through", said the bird. Once she had hauled the mouse out onto the seed platform, the bright eyed bird introduced herself.

"Hi! My name is DeeDee Chickadee. I happened to be in the lilac bush next to Rufus' house when you arrived this morning, so I overheard your plans. Rufus is a good friend of ours. So any friend of his is a friend of ours, right Peter

Peter?"

"Right right, peter peter!" answered the tufted titmouse.

"By the way, I'd like to introduce you to a friend of mine. This is Peter Peter Tufted Titmouse. And your name is?

"Toddy Fieldmouse."

Peter Peter hopped over and extended a wing to Toddy. She took it carefully in her paw. The feathers were slender and silky. As she stood there, she thought in amazement. "So far today I've shaken paws with a bullfrog, a dog and now a tufted titmouse, and the day's not even over yet!"

Peter Peter looked at Toddy a moment, and then he spoke.

"Come right-ight this way, and have something to eat eat eat. Do you favor crack-ack corn or plump-ump raisins?"

"Corn would be fine," replied Toddy as she walked behind the two birds. She wondered why Peter Peter repeated himself so much, but not wishing to be impolite, she did not ask. She was also beginning to wonder why every bird she had met so far, including Jay Jay, said their name twice.

"Perhaps it's a bird thing," she thought.

Her thoughts changed *abruptly* when he noticed a tail sticking out of a pile of cracked corn.

"Herb!" called Dee Dee.

No answer.

"Herb, we have company!"

Still no answer.

Peter Peter hopped over to the protruding tail, took it in his beak, and gave a gentle tug.

Up popped a mouse somewhat larger than Toddy. His cheeks were full of cracked corn. He chewed, gulped, and looked at Peter Peter.

"What's up?" *queried* Herb.

"We have company – ompany," said Peter Peter, nodding his head in the direction of Toddy. Herb turned and what he saw was a mouse in a hat. That by itself made him stare, but the fact that she was a field mouse made her a curiosity.

Herb had never been outside the safe walls of the sanctuary. He was a stone wall mouse. He lived each day relatively free from cats, hawks, and other predators. Herb continued to stare until Dee Dee broke the silence.

"Toddy, I'd like you to meet Herb G. Mouse, a resident of our community. Herb, this is Toddy Fieldmouse. She's come with Bunny Pufftail to watch the pumpkin carving festivities. You remember meeting Bunny Pufftail last spring, don't you? How about you two dining together while Peter Peter and I partake of some sunflower seeds?"

"That would be fine," said Toddy. "I'm so hungry right now that I could even eat a pumpkin."

Peter Peter chuckled, "I come from a long line of pumpkin eaters. Why, my great great-grandfather Peter Peter had a poem written about his pumpkin eating ability-ilities. History didn't get it straight, though. He only ate the seeds. Speak-eaking of seeds, lets stop all this talk-alking and eat eat eat! See you later baked pertater."

"After a while, smoochy smile," Herb responded. The two birds hopped off in the direction of the sunflower seeds, leaving the mice to themselves.

"Smoochy smile?" asked Toddy as she began nibbling on the cracked corn.

"Just a rhyming game we play with each other. We try to finish one another's rhymes with a silly ending."

"May I ask you a question?" Toddy asked.

"If it's the meaning of smoochy smile, I'm afraid there is none," said Herb.

"No. I was wondering what the G stood for in your middle name," Toddy replied.

Herb chuckled. "You won't believe it, but it stands for garden."

"You're right, I don't believe it," laughed Toddy, almost spitting out a mouthful of cracked corn. "Herb Garden?"

"Momma names us for the plants that we're born under. I was born between a patch of parsley and rosemary.

Since neither name seemed suitable for a boy mouse, Momma came up with the idea of Herb Garden."

"I am glad you weren't born in the asparagus patch," chuckled Toddy.

"Or amongst the zucchinis," laughed Herb. "May I ask you a question now?"

"Please do," replied Toddy.

"Where is your friend Bunny Pufftail?"

"At the gazebo eating lunch, I believe. Rufus took her there. They should be returning fairly soon."

"I like your hat," said Herb as he popped corn into his mouth. "How'd you come by it?"

"Bunny Pufftail found it on the old farm road last year. She made inquires all around, but no one seemed to know where it came from, so she brought it home to High Meadow thinking that we mice might like it. We held a *raffle* for it and I won."

Suddenly Jay Jay gave a loud call from the top of a

hemlock tree.

"They're here, they're here!

Let's give a cheer!

The pumpkin carvers are drawing near!"

Sharon Pape '07

Chapter Eight
Observations

At the signal, all the birds flocked to the trees. All except for Dee Dee and Peter Peter, that is.

As Plumy and her mom pulled an old rusty wagon into the bird sanctuary, more than fifty pairs of eyes watched from the trees above.

"It's pumpkin carving time. It's pumpkin carving time" chanted the birds.

Rufus and Bunny Pufftail followed a safe distance behind the wagon. Finally Bunny Pufftail said, "Rufus, you'd better go on ahead. Plumy is expecting you. I'll take the bush route and meet you by the clump of lilacs. Can you get word to Jay Jay?"

"Certainly," replied Rufus. "What do you want him to do?"

"I'd like him to tell Toddy where I am. As soon as Plumy is done with the pumpkin carving, we need to head for High Meadow. It's going to take us longer to get home than I thought, since we won't be able to take the frog ferry on the return trip. I'd like to get us home before nightfall. Don't want to meet up with the coyote clan."

Rufus stood for a moment, deep in thought. Then he spoke. "I've got an idea, but I have to discuss it with someone first before I tell you about it. I'll call Jay Jay for you."

Rufus gave three quick barks and Jay Jay appeared. The old dog muttered something into the bird's ear and Bunny Pufftail politely stepped back so as to avoid *eavesdropping*. She could tell by Jay Jay's *intent* expression that big plans were about to unfold. Rufus turned to Bunny Pufftail and said, "Jay Jay is going to show you a secret way to get close to the Ott ladies without being seen. Hopefully, it will make my plan work as well. See you in a bit." With that, the dog again set his propeller tail in motion and headed out of the sanctuary.

Jay Jay flew over to where Bunny Pufftail stood and said cheerfully, "Are you ready for some high adventure, with the emphasis on high?"

Bunny Pufftail gave him a puzzled look and said, "I don't know what Rufus' plan is, but I'm ready if you are."

"I'm going to show you how to hop up on the stone wall that surrounds this place," said the bird.

"There's a picnic table next to it that you can use as stairs. Once you're on top of the wall you can use it as a road. It'll take you to where the Ott gals are without bein' seen. They'll be too busy carvin' the pumpkin to look up. From there, you'll be able to see Toddy. I'll zip back and forth with messages whenever you like."

"That's a fine plan Rufus has *conceived*. He's one smart *canine*," said Bunny Pufftail.

"And he's one smart dog too," replied Jay Jay.

Meanwhile the "Ott gals," as Jay Jay liked to call them, had come to a halt with their load directly beneath the feeder where Toddy was dining.

"Was that Rufus barking?" asked Mrs. Ott.

"He was calling Jay Jay," answered Plumy.

"Jay Jay?"

"You know, Mommy, the piggy blue jay who eats sunflower seeds," said Plumy.

"Ah yes, the seed eater extraordinaire. Why was Rufus calling Jay Jay?" she asked as she began placing newspapers on the ground.

"I think it is confidential," said Plumy quietly.

"And what does 'confidential' mean?" asked Mrs. Ott teasingly.

"You said it means top secret or nobody's beeswax." she replied.

"Ah yesa, so I dida," she chuckled. "Wella Pluma Rachel, bambino of the juicy wordsa, coma helpa youra mama lifta this biga pumpa ken!" (Mrs. Ott loved to speak pretend Italian, and used it at every opportunity with her family. It produced tremendous eye rolling, especially from Mr. Ott.)

"Yesa Mama mia," laughed Plumy as she grabbed the bottom of the pumpkin and lifted it out of the wagon. She placed it down in the center of the newspapers and pulled a purple crayon out from her sweater pocket.

"While you draw on the face that you want, I'm going over and tip the picnic table on its side. We won't be using it any more this year, and it will help to keep the snow from piling up on the top."

"Okay Mommy."

"Holey Moley," said Jay Jay. "How are you going to get off this stone wall if she takes away the picnic table?"

"Well, I can't fly down, that's for sure," said Bunny Pufftail.

"I'm sure that Rufus will have a plan when he gets back.

Panicking certainly won't do me any good. So I might as well sit back and enjoy the festivities. Would you go tell Toddy of the situation, Jay Jay?"

"Well, dog my kitties, if you aren't the bravest bunny I ever knew."

"I'm not that brave," said Bunny Pufftail. "I just try to think things through a bit. Saves my feet a lot of unnecessary hopping. I've had my panicking moments though. Got caught in a field with a big snake once. Almost sprouted wings I jumped so high."

Jay Jay cackled as he thought of the *image*.

"Sprouted wings! That's a good one," he laughed. "Guess I'll sprout mine and go see Toddy."

In two short hops he was airborne. Hearing Jay Jay overhead, Plumy looked up just in time to see Bunny Pufftail crouching on the wall. She *averted* her eyes quickly as her mother came back. Jay Jay landed on the feeder with a bounce.

"Hey there, Jay Jay!" called Mrs. Ott. "Save some seeds

for the rest of the gang, okay? Are you ready to carve, Plume?"

"Yes, Mommy. I didn't draw any curves like last year though. I remember how hard it was for you to cut."

"Well, this year you can make as many curves as you want. I bought a real pumpkin knife at the store. Guaranteed to cut easily and it's finger friendly to boot."

"How about triangles for the eyes and nose, and a wiggly smile?" asked Plumy.

"Sounds good to me," said Mrs. Ott. "I'll cut the lid out so you can start taking out the guts."

"Yuck!" said Plumy, wrinkling her face in *mock* disgust.

"Sorry, I couldn't resist," laughed Mrs. Ott.

In a few minutes her mother had cut around the stem and pulled the lid off. As Plumy reached in and pulled out the seeds and *membranes*, she spread them out on the newspapers to dry.

While Bunny Pufftail did her best to look like a rock on

the wall, Toddy and Herb peered over the edge of the seed platform with the three birds.

Plumy took quick secret glances at Bunny Pufftail as she continued cleaning out the pumpkin. She smiled to herself at the thought of her mystery guests. "I wonder where Toddy is, though?" she thought.

Mrs. Ott saw the *quizzical* look on her daughter's face and said, "Anything wrong, Plumy?"

"Not really. Just wondering about a mouse," she replied.

"What about a mouse?" her mother asked.

"I was wondering if it likes pumpkin seeds."

"I doubt if mice ever get the opportunity to eat pumpkin seeds. Even if they lived right next door to a whole field of pumpkins, they'd still need to have the jaws of a shark to chew their way through the shell. If you'd like, we could stick some seeds in the cracks of the stone wall. Seems like I've seen a mouse or two over there when I was weeding. You know, I had a mouse friend when I was your age."

"Really?" asked Plumy, her eyes widening.

"I was picking vegetables for your grandma and there she was. I named her Parsnip."

"I thought you didn't like mice," said Plumy, suddenly alert to her mom's every word.

"Well, I don't want them dancing on my head, but I do enjoy watching nature unfold around me. Even bugs and spiders are a marvel. As your grandma used to say to me, 'All life is a miracle.'"

"I like the name Parsnip," said Plumy. "Speaking of names, how come Jay Jay's name is a double?"

"Simple really," replied her mother. "That's his call. When a blue jay calls out, he says 'jay jay.' When a crow calls, he says 'caw caw.' If you were a woodpecker you'd call yourself 'Tatty Tatty.' It's just a quick way of identifying who's who."

"If a chicken lived in the sanctuary, she'd be called Cluck Cluck?" asked Plumy.

"I guess!" laughed her mother.

"How about a cow?" her daughter asked grinning.

"Moo Moo, of course, but only if it was wearing wings," chuckled her mother.

"That solves the mystery of Dee Dee and Peter Peter's names," thought Toddy as she listened and watched *intently* from her perch.

Jay Jay hopped over next to Toddy and said, "I think you'd better skeedaddle pretty soon 'cause by the time you reach where Bunny Pufftail is, Rufus'll be there waitin' on the outside of the wall with Bucksnort."

"Bucksnort?" questioned Toddy, her eyes widening.

"Oh stinkbugs! Me and my babbling beak! I wasn't supposed to tell you that, bein' that it's a surprise and all. Well, toodledoo surprise!"

"Bucksnort. Is that a dog friend of Rufus?" asked Toddy.

"Not exactly," said Jay Jay. "Friend, yes. Dog, no. I'll say no more."

Herb turned towards Toddy and spoke in a quiet voice. "I know a quick route to the stone wall. It would be my pleasure to accompany you there. I need to be getting home anyway since I have to start cleaning out the winter store-room."

Toddy looked up at Herb and said, "I appreciate the escort, Herb. Please lead the way."

The two mice walked over to the birds to say their goodbyes.

"Come again, Toddy Fieldmouse when you can stay longer," said Dee Dee. "It's been a delight meeting you."

"Yes yes yes," said Peter Peter. "Come again anytime anytime." And turning toward Herb, he said, "Toodledoo to both of you."

Herb replied with a grin, "Have a nice day, I wish we could stay."

Chapter Nine
High Adventure

As the two mice turned to leave, Jay Jay, all perky with curiosity, hopped over to Herb's side.

"You takin' Toddy on the high wire skeedoodle?"

Before Herb could reply or give an explanation to Toddy, Jay Jay turned towards her and blurted out, "I sure hope you aren't scared of heights, 'cause the skeedoodle is one **wild** ride! 'Course Tommy Squirrel will be there if anything should go wrong. Not that anything'll go wrong mind you, but accidents do happen and . . .

His voice trailed off as he caught sight of Herb's face and Toddy's wide-eyed expression.

"What? What?" inquired the puzzled bird.

"Nothing, Nothing, Jay Jay," replied Herb. He did not wish to encourage the bird to further discussion. Toddy's eyes were wide enough, and she was beginning to twist her tail, a sure sign of mouse nerves.

"Just waiting for you to take a breath, my blue feathered fellow. Come on Toddy, we're going to ride the suet tram or as Jay Jay here likes to call it, 'the highwire skeedoodle'."

Extending over the seed platform and surrounding the maple tree was a small, well-made, shingled roof that protected the seed piles during *inclement* weather. It was to this roof that Herb now led Toddy. A wood vine twirled its way around one of the roof posts and made a fine ladder for the mice to climb.

Jay Jay, finally realizing that his audience was leaving, hopped after them talking as he went. "High wire skeedoodle sounds so much more interestin' than suet tram don't you think Toddy? I mean suet tram sounds downright greasy. Isn't that what suet is? Big chunks of greasy fat? Who'd want to ride in that? Maybe a woodpecker perhaps, but that's about it. Yeesh! On the other hand, high wire skeedoodle sounds *majestic*, impressive, adventuresome, and throws in the tiniest hint of danger for good measure." As he said this, his bright little eyes squinted for dramatic effect. "Tommy squirrel said his business has doubled since I renamed it," said Jay Jay, proudly puffing out his chest.

The bird took one hopping flap and landed on the roof just as Toddy and Herb finished climbing the wood vine.

"Tommy, Tommy!" called Jay Jay. "You've got customers! Shake a leg, shake a tail!"

Tommy squirrel, hearing his name, scrambled paw over paw on a pulley clothesline that was attached to the roof's corner and where the trio now stood. From this roof corner the clothesline extended over to the stone wall where Bunny Pufftail remained *stranded*. At that end the clothesline was attached to a pole near Herb's doorway in the stone wall. In the winter, Mrs. Ott hung the suet feeders on the clothesline for the woodpeckers as Jay Jay had said, but, from May to early November they hung empty since suet will spoil in warm weather. These feeders resembled small cages and Tommy ran them back and forth from June to the end of October. Chipmunks and mice paid him one acorn apiece for a *leisurely* ride to and from the seed platform. The more thrill-seeking rodents paid double for a speedier run. Jay Jay had conceived the idea and helped Tommy collect the acorns from the paying customers.

Tommy dropped down from the clothesline and landed directly in front of the two mice. His whiskers drooped like the boughs of a Christmas tree overloaded with ornaments. Droplets of a mysterious brown goo clung from each whisker and when he smiled he displayed two very brown teeth!

"Been at the peanut butter again, I see," laughed Jay Jay. "Looks like you went swimmin' in it."

Tommy continued to smile and attempted to clean his

face with his paws. Finally he extended his paw to Toddy but quickly withdrew it when he realized how sticky it was.

"Thorry about that," said Tommy. "I juth had lunth with Luthy at the peanut butter feeder. Luthys' my wife, you know. Ith's the firth thime we've had a sthpare moment to ourthelvths thinth the kidth were born. Luthy and I've had our pawth full all thummer teathen 'em the wayth of the thwirrel. Haven't even been able to athend any OQR meetinths thinth thith patht April!"

"OQR?" inquired Toddy, giving Herb a questioning look.

"Order of the Quick Rodents," replied Jay Jay before Herb could answer. "Tommy, have you got peanut butter stuck to the roof of your mouth? 'Cause your words sound glued together. How 'bout you eaten' a nice pinecone or somethin' while I keep Toddy and Herb entertained?

Smiling broadly, Tommy's upper lip became stuck to his upper teeth. He wiggled his whiskers and twitched his nose to free it, but finally had to extract his lip with his paws. Bowing and backing away, Tommy politely excused himself. Leaping up, he grabbed on to the nearest suet basket that dangled from the lower loop of the clothesline. With his added weight and force the basket began to drop away from the seed platform, gathering speed as it soared over the heads of the two Otts. They barely looked up, as they were used to Tommy's *shenanigans.* Bunny Pufftail on the other hand couldn't take her eyes of the *careening* squirrel. She was about to yell "Watch out for the pole!" when Tommy suddenly let go of the basket. He made a perfect four pawed landing while the suet basket banged into the pole with a loud whack! The Otts looked up casually while Tommy scampered off towards the pine trees in search of a pine cone toothbrush.

Mrs. Ott smirked and said "One of these days that squirrel is going to crash into that pole and shake his teeth loose."

"I don't think so, Mommy," said Plumy. "Why, Tommy is the best high wire skeedoodler there is. Rufus even says so. He's a real acrobat!"

Mrs. Ott chuckled and said, "I suppose you're right, Plumy. I guess he should be, after all the practice he gets. Perhaps we should call in the circus people. Of course Tommy would want to be paid in peanut butter and that might be so costly that it would probably put the circus right out of business!"

Bunny Pufftail chuckled to herself at the idea of Tommy joining the circus. She could just imagine him wearing a sparkling *sequined* cape swinging on a tiny trapeze high about the crowds. Many's the time that she and Uncle Edward had slipped away during the summer months to see the circus when it was in a field nearby. The high wire acts were always her favorite.

As Plumy and her mother carved the last snarly tooth on the jack-o-lantern, Tommy squirrel suddenly came *bounding* across the grass directly in their path. In his haste to return to his customers, he had clearly forgotten they were there. At the last second he tucked in his plumed tail, leaped over the jack-o-lantern, and hit the ground running. Without stopping he scurried up the post to the feeding platform. It happened so quickly that Plumy and her mother didn't have time to react.

"Well that's the first time I've had a close encounter of a squirrel kind," laughed Mrs. Ott, falling backward into the grass. "On that note let's get this mess cleaned up and take our pumpkin friend here to the porch before Tommy decides to give us another thrill."

They proceeded to clean up the area, left the seeds to dry on a large wooden tray and hauled the jack-o-lantern away in the wagon.

Meanwhile, Toddy and Herb climbed aboard the second suet cage and waited for Tommy to push off. The first cage Tommy had used when he had gone to brush his teeth, hung from the bottom rope of the clothesline. The one in which Toddy and Herb were now *ensconced* hung from the top rope.

Mrs. Ott had *suspended* the two cages in this way so that when she pulled on the clothesline, one cage came toward her and the other one departed. She had done this *solely* for the convenience of Tommy. This way he didn't have to retrieve a cage between shuttles, for there were always mice coming and going at both ends.

"I have no acorns with me to pay for the ride, Tommy," said Herb. "But I have something back at my home that I think you would like even better. I can run in and get them after you drop us off at the stone wall."

"What is it?" asked Tommy, his nose suddenly all twitchy with excitement.

"Two bags of salted peanuts. Never been opened." replied the mouse.

Tommy's eyes began to glaze over and he clutched his

paws to his chest. "Heart be still and fur be smooth," exclaimed the squirrel. "Won't Lucy be thrilled!?" he declared. He knew that once the children got a whiff of the opened bag, there would be no peace in the nest until every last nut was gobbled up and gone! Of course, they would save the other bag for a cold winter's night. But tonight, tonight! There would be serious nibbling!

Quickly, Tommy reached up and grabbed the cage that held Toddy and Herb. Once again the high wire skeedoodle lurched forward, picking up speed as it *surged* forth toward the opposite clothes pole.

Toddy clutched the sides of the cage while Herb sat behind her, seemingly relaxed. Her whiskers tensed as Tommy began climbing to the bottom of the suet basket and just as she was about to ask Herb how Tommy was going to slow the ride down, the squirrel suddenly hooked his feet into the bottom of the cage and hung upside down! To Bunny Pufftail below, he looked like the catcher in the trapeze act she had seen with Uncle Edward. Stretching to his full length, Tommy grabbed the lower loop of the clothesline with his claws. This action had the result of a set of brakes and slowed their speed down by half. He had quickly learned not to grip the rope with his paws. The first and only time he had mistakenly done so resulted in a rope burn that had forced him to shut the ride down for a month.

Tommy let go of the rope for a fleeting moment to allow the lower line suet basket to pass by. It was filled with three mice on their way to the main seed platform. This basket would arrive at exactly the same time as Herb and Toddy's basket would, for Mrs. Ott had cleverly hung the two baskets enough apart so that each reached their destinations precisely at the same moment.

Toddy caught a *fleeting* glance of the three mice in the lower basket. They appeared to be blind, for each had a cane and oddly enough each was wearing a pair of dark sunglasses.

"Why are those mice wearing dark glasses?" she asked Herb.

"They're blind," he replied. "They like to eat at the platform. Been doin' it for years. They're neighbors of mine, live a couple rocks down from me in the stone wall. Mrs. Ott feeds 'em in the winter so they don't have to forage outside."

"That Mrs. Ott seems especially kind to us animal folk," replied Toddy.

"Mrs. Ott is an outstanding human," remarked Herb. "There's nothing that any one of us wouldn't do for her. She's a *saint* in my book. Some day when you visit us again, I'll tell you some more stories about her. She grew up in this house you see, and when she married Mr. Ott they decided to stay on and work the farm with her dad. She knows every *nook* and *cranny* around here. Saved many of our lives in one way or another. You know how we're taught to be invisible around people? Well, with Mrs. Ott you needn't worry. Nor with Plumy either. They're good folk."

"What about Mr. Ott?" asked Toddy?

"Oh, he's alright, though I tend to steer clear of him because of his big feet. He doesn't always watch were he's steppin' like Mrs. Ott and Plumy do."

Herb and Toddy's attention returned to Tommy as he continued to slow the basket down with his claws. Finally when the basket came to a stop, Tommy pushed it snugly against the clothesline pulley. While he held it there firmly with his paws, Herb loosened the suet cage door. The two mice then made a dash over the crosspiece of the pulley to the clothes pole, which was made of a cedar tree. The bark covered pole made it fairly easy for Herb and Tommy to climb down. Two minutes later they were back on good old earth and one minute after that Tommy was standing next to them.

Chapter Ten
Departure

Bunny Pufftail leaned over the stone wall and called down to Toddy. "How was your trip?" she inquired.

"Terrifying, but I'd do it all over again," laughed Toddy. "I wish you could have come with us."

"Well, to borrow a human expression, 'I wish that I could have been a mouse in your pocket.' Unfortunately I'd make too big a mouse!" chuckled Bunny Pufftail. "I had a good time watching you two though. Speaking of two, when are you going to introduce me to your two friends here?"

Toddy opened her mouth to reply but suddenly Jay Jay landed on the wall next to Bunny Pufftail. "That's Herb Mouse and that's Tommy Squirrel, two friends of mine," declared the bird.

"Two friends of Toddy's as well," said Rufus sternly coming up behind the group. "And she was just about to introduce them when you interrupted her, Jay Jay."

The group jumped in shock at the sound of Rufus' unexpected voice.

"When did you get here?" asked Jay Jay quickly recovering from his shock.

"A few moments ago, but don't be changing the subject Jay Jay," replied Rufus gruffly.

Jay Jay gulped and seemed to shrink in size. He felt miserable. Why couldn't he just keep his beak shut he wondered? Giving Toddy a *remorseful* look, the *enthusiasm* Jay Jay had shown a minute before seemed to drain right down out of his drooping tail.

"I'm sorry, Toddy", said the *contrite* bird. "I don't mean to blurt things out so. I just get so excited sometimes that I can't stop talking."

"It's alright, Jay Jay. I've been known to get excited too," said Toddy.

"Really?" asked Jay Jay.

"Really really!" laughed Toddy.

"Let's just say Jay Jay is highly *exuberant*" said Rufus, arching his eyebrows toward the bird.

"What's exer-brunt?" asked Jay Jay curiously.

"It's exuberant, Jay Jay, and it means enthusiastic, or joyously unrestrained" replied Rufus. "Come to think of it, that's a pretty fair description of me when I was a young one. I got off my leash a few times as a pup and I'd say that joyously unrestrained described me to a T. I even ended up in a wonderful mud puddle once." The old dog chuckled at the memory. "I guess that I should be a bit more tolerant of your outbursts Jay Jay. You know the saying."

"Take the branch out of your own eye so that you can see well enough to remove the twig from the other bird's eye?" asked Jay Jay.

"Something like that" replied Rufus smiling.

"Shouldn't we be letting these folks get on home?" asked Tommy interrupting. "It's getting late and they should leave if they want to get home by nightfall. Don't mean to rush you folks, but there are a lot of dangers lurking in the dark."

"You're right, Tommy" replied Herb. "And I heard Mr.Ott say that it was going to rain."

"I guess it's time that I sprouted those wings that I mentioned earlier, Jay Jay" said Bunny Pufftail. I don't see how I'm going to get off this wall otherwise. Rufus, would you mind giving Toddy a ride back up to High Meadow? Tell the folks up there that I'll be along when I can".

"But you don't have to," blurted Jay Jay.

"Sprout wings?" puzzled Bunny Pufftail.

"What Jay Jay is trying to say in his exuberant way" said Rufus, *interceding*, "Is that you don't have to be stuck on the wall and I don't need to escort Toddy. Bucksnort is here".

"Bucksnort?" queried Toddy and Bunny Pufftail together.

"Bucksnort, Bucksnort" cheered the birds when they heard the name. Suddenly Jay Jay flew up to the stone wall and took a position by Bunny Pufftail. Facing the birds that were now perched at attention on every feeder and branch, Jay Jay raised his wings as if he was about to conduct an orchestra. What followed was a *rousing* cheer.

Who's a friend to all right here?

Bucksnort Bucksnort

What a deer!

Saves us from the hawks on high

Bucksnort Bucksnort

He's our guy!

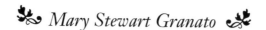

Stamps his hoof when cats are near

Bucksnort Bucksnort

Give a cheer!

Snorts at danger, flags his tail

Bucksnort, Bucksnort

Will not fail!

Weasels fear him, foxes too,

Bucksnort Bucksnort

We love you!

Suddenly a large rack of antlers followed by a big brown head rose up from the other side of the stone wall near where Bunny Pufftail now stood.

"Did I just hear someone call my name?" said Bucksnort.

Immediately about fifteen birds flew down from their perches, settled on his antlers and began singing their happiest songs.

With a *bewildered* look, Toddy turned towards Herb. Herb just grinned back and said, "You mean that you weren't expecting to see a deer with a rack of birds on his head? It is startling at first, I'll admit, but we're so used to it that we forget how extraordinary it must appear to outsiders. However, Bucksnort is no ordinary deer. Ever since he was a young buck he has been a friend to all of us at the sanctuary. If a bird or mouse happens to be outside these protective walls, Bucksnort keeps an eye out for him or her and if he senses danger, he lifts his tail in warning. Why, he even gives us rides back to the safety of the sanctuary! In the winter Mr.Ott throws out hay bales for him on the sunny side of the barn. He even lets him hang out with cows during hunting season! He's a remarkable fellow."

"Who, Mr. Ott or Bucksnort?" inquired Toddy with a little smile.

"Hah! I see your point. How about both of them?" laughed Herb.

At that moment Bucksnort looked over the stone wall at Rufus and said, "I'm ready to hit the trail whenever your friends are."

Jay Jay hopped closer to Bunny Pufftail and spoke before the old dog could respond. "This is the famous Bucksnort that I spoke of earlier. He's a dear deer friend and he's going to be your taxi home."

"Jay Jay, please don't refer to me as a taxi," said the deer. "It sounds too much like *taxidermy* and I'm not ready to be stuffed as of yet. How about deer mobile or buck-board? Or you could call me a cab, a carriage, a coach, a conveyance or a surrey with the fringe on top", he snorted. "Just don't use the T word."

"Your exuberance is showing again Jay Jay. But I'm thinking that Bucksnort is having a little fun with words at your expense," said Rufus smiling. "Perhaps he's feeling a little exuberant as well".

"Could be. Could be that I am," laughed Bucksnort. "By the way Rufus, you don't have to contend with the *hooligans* that have been smashing Mr. Ott's pumpkins anymore."

"Oh?" questioned Rufus.

"I was out for a moonlit walk the other night. I couldn't sleep. A bunch of tough looking kids were having **quite** the time of it. That is until I gave them one of my best snorts followed by a few well placed stamps on the ground. I was hiding in the bushes at the time. I think that those *scoundrels* thought I was some kind of wild animal. Come to think of it, I am! At any rate Halloween came a little early for them this year. They wanted to trick so I *countered* with a treat. The whole lot of them took off as if they'd seen a ghost. For my own amusement I even bellowed. I haven't done that in years."

"Bucksnort, I owe you one", said Rufus. "I have been trying to catch those *varmints* for quite some time but they only seem to come out and do their dirty work at night after I have been put on my chain."

"You don't owe me a thing, Rufus. Your friendship and kindness towards us wild folk is payment enough," replied Bucksnort.

"Thank you Bucksnort," said Rufus *humbly*.

"Toddy, it's time that you said your good-byes to everyone and get up on the wall with Bunny Pufftail. There are plenty of ivy vines to use to get you there," said Rufus.

Toddy turned and extended her paw first to Herb and then to Tommy. "Thank you so much for showing me such a wonderful time. The lunch was delicious and the high wire skeedoodle was everything that Jay Jay said it would be and then some. I can't wait to come back in the spring. Maybe my sister Rhonda can come then as well. Perhaps you could come to High Meadow and visit us sometime? I'll see if it's alright with my family."

"You and Bunny Pufftail are welcome here anytime,"

said Herb. "I think that I speak for all of us when I say that any of your kin are welcome here too. As far as visiting you at High Meadow, I can't make any promises; but I thank you for the invitation"

Toddy turned to Rufus and as a final farewell, climbed up on his foot and hugged him around the leg. Neither dog nor mouse could speak. The dog leaned down and *nuzzled* her head. Everyone waited politely. Finally in a voice so soft that only Rufus could hear, Toddy whispered in his ear. The dog smiled and said, "I feel the same way about you, Toddy."Then as quickly as she had come, Toddy hopped off and scampered up the nearest ivy vine, her hat dangling from her neck. When she finally made it to the top of the wall, Toddy stepped near the edge and peered down at Rufus.

"I forgot to give you something that I think may belong to Plumy. Would you see that she gets it?" And with that Toddy removed her straw hat and tossed it down to the dog.

"I'll take it to her today personally, and I thank you for it on her behalf. Good-bye Mousie, till we meet again"

Toddy smiled at the use of her pet name, waved, and turned to Bunny Pufftail. "Ready to go?" she asked.

Just then Jay Jay stepped up and interrupted, but this time he said "Pardon my *intrusion* folks, but would it be alright if I tagged along with you and Bucksnort a ways? I have some relatives that I've been meanin' to visit before winter comes. I've been so busy around here with my *guardianship* duties I haven't had a chance to get away."

"I'm thinking that you also would like some traveling companions," said Bucksnort. "Or could I be mistaken?"

Jay Jay gave him his best saucy look and cocked his head to one side. "Been takin' up mind readin' in your spare time there, Bucksnort? 'Cause if you have, you're gettin' pretty good at it," said the bird, grinning.

"Hop aboard everyone," said Bucksnort as he bent his head down to the level of the stone wall. "For safety reasons

I think it's best if you all find your favorite antler and hang on. I'm afraid that I don't come equipped with seatbelts."

Jay Jay quickly flew up and perched on the highest antler so as to act as look out while Bunny Pufftail and Toddy positioned themselves between the two main branches that came off the top of Bucksnort's head. Anyone looking from a distance would have thought that the deer was wearing some kind of fur hat.

The birds of the sanctuary sang their best songs of farewell and some of the stone wall mice waved as Bucksnort began to stride gracefully through the field toward High Meadow and home.

Epilogue

That evening as Mrs. Ott was tucking Plumy in for the night, she noticed a doll's straw hat on the nightstand next to her daughter's bed. She also noticed five pumpkin seeds drying on a tissue next to it.

"What are you doing with the seeds Plume? Are you planning on having a midnight snack with some mice?" inquired her mom.

"Well, I was thinking about how neat it would be to plant some of the seeds from our jack-o-lantern next spring to grow a new batch of pumpkins. We could do the same thing every year. What do you think?"

"I think that is a great idea. It will be a *perpetual*

pumpkin that way", replied her mother.

"What does perpetual mean, Mommy?"

"Why don't we look it up together tomorrow, since it's time for all good daughters to snuggle down and go to sleep?"

"Okay", said Plumy as her mother pulled the blankets up under her chin.

As her mother leaned over to turn out the light on the nightstand, she gave the straw hat a second look.

"Where did that come from Plumy? Isn't that the doll hat that you lost last spring?"

"Rufus brought it to me tonight Mommy, just before Daddy took him out to his doghouse."

"That's odd", said her mother. "It appears to have a couple of holes in the brim. I wonder who made them. Could it be a *pooka*?"

"If that's another word for mouse then I think you're right, Mommy."

Mrs. Ott gave her daughter a knowing smile and said "You know, this hat could tell quite a tale if it could talk. Perhaps tomorrow you could write a story about it."

And the very next day Pluma Rachel Ott did. She called it <u>Toddy Mouse and the Everlasting Pumpkin.</u>

GLOSSARY

Pufftails Pointers for Parents
italics...... a style of slanted writing started in the fourteen hundreds.

Chapter One

stubble...... the short grass still attached to the roots after mowing
mammoth......very large, enormous, huge
periscopes...... a long, tube shaped instrument that submarines use to see above the water.
inseparable......always together, not able to be separated
equivalent......same as or identical
investigate...... to search or question in order to understand or learn
    something
miniature...... small in scale
predators...... animals that live by hunting and eating other animals
fatal......deadly
duo.....a pair or two companions
hastened......hurried or went quickly

Chapter Two

looming......towering over
churning......stirring violently or boiling
commotion......noisy disturbance
cockeyed......off center, tilted at an angle
trepidation......fear
hoisted......lifted
rowdy......rough or tough
rodents......animals that have front teeth that are chisel shaped for
    gnawing bark, nuts or hard woody surfaces.
banned......not allowed, prohibited

hoard......treasure or bounty

tufts......a growing bunch of grasses or close set plants

protruding......sticking out

camouflaged......disguised in order to blend into the surroundings

stationed......positioned

niche......a recessed spot or nook in a wall or hole

massive......huge or large

stern......the back end of a boat

toadstool......mushroom

recessed......hidden

nestled......settled snugly or comfortably

reputation......a quality or character seen or judged by most people

integrity......honesty

moral......virtuous, noble

Chapter Three

loped...... moved or ran in an easy manner

fragrance......a sweet or delicate smell or scent

emerged......come out from

exotic......strange or unusual to the area, foreign or not native to the
   place where found

inquired......investigated, asked around

obediently...... doing what you are asked to do willingly

steed......a horse (usually high spirited)

propelling......driving forward

thrust......forward push

trespassers......intruders or uninvited people

pursuit......the act of following

Chapter Four

stowaways...... those who hide in a vehicle in order to get a free ride

authority......power, influence

encountered......met face to face

conquering......overcoming, becoming victorious

regretted......was very sorry for

gargantuan......of tremendous size

clambered......climbed awkwardly, scrambled

introductions......exchanging greetings and names when first meeting

awestruck......filled with wonder or amazement

confident......sure, certain

recognition......the action of noticing and remembering someone from before

dialects......manners of speech and pronunciations of language

concentrated......focusing your attention on one thing or task

advancing......moving or proceeding forward

laden......loaded or burdened

serene......calm, peaceful

Chapter Five

frantically......behaving with great urgency or out of control

outcroppings......part of a rock formation that appears at the surface

ordeal......a difficult or severe experience

squeamish......queasy stomach or nauseous

lurched......rolled, jerked or tipped abruptly

accompanied......went with someone as a companion

escort......to go with someone to protect them

sanctuary......a place of refuge and protection

plaintively......with suffering or sadness in manner or voice

inquiries......requests for information

intercede......to intervene or act as a mediator between opposing groups in order to solve a problem

foreign......from another country or strange in character or behavior

hospitality......friendly welcome towards others

quenched......to relieve or satisfy with liquid

appalling......inspiring dismay or disgust

unison......at the same time

trio......a group of three
concealed......hidden
gazebo......freestanding roofed structure, usually open on two sides
hovering......to remain suspended over a place or object

Chapter Six

saucy......bold
extraordinaire......going beyond what is usual or regular
inquisitive......curious
imminent......ready to take place or about to happen
spectacle......eye catching or dramatic public display
dramatic......acting out as if on stage
engrossed......totally occupied with something
loquacious......talkative
impose......burden with, force upon, take advantage of
dependability......trustworthy, can be relied upon, steadfast
independence......freedom
apprehension......fear, anxiety
veritable......real, genuine, authentic

Chapter Seven

foraging...... the act of wandering about in search of food
contemplating......pondering, considering or thinking about
abruptly......suddenly
queried......asked
curiosity......desire to know
raffle......a lottery where a prize is won by many people buying
    chances

Chapter Eight

eavesdropping......listening secretly to what is said in private
intent......purpose, plan
conceived......created

canine......of or relating to dogs
image......idea, concept or picture
averted......turn away or aside (as the eyes), avoid
mock......pretend or artificial
membranes......thin soft layers of either animal or plant origin
quizzical......puzzled
intently......concentrated or eager attention to someone or something

Chapter Nine

inclement...... severe or stormy as in weather
majestic......grand, noble
stranded......stuck or left in a place without means to leave
leisurely......unhurried or relaxed
shenanigans......mischievous or devious behavior
careening......lurching forward, descending quickly
sequined......fabric covered in a decoration of very small and very
    shiny plastic or metal coin shapes so as to give off sparkle
bounding......leaping or jumping
ensconced.....concealed or established
suspended......hanging down
solely......for one purpose or by one's self
surged......roll forward
fleeting......passing swiftly
saint-a person officially recognized as being holy, sacred or good
nook......a sheltered spot or recess
cranny......unknown or hard to find crack or crevice in a wall

Chapter Ten

remorseful......full of guilt
enthusiasm......eagerness
contrite......sorry
exuberant......joyously unrestrained
interceding...... coming between people to solve differences

rousing......lively or stirring

bewildered......confused

taxidermy......the art of stuffing and mounting animal skins or
    bodies

contend......deal or struggle with

hooligans......ruffians, hoodlums, bullies, or thugs

scoundrels......villains or rascals

countered......opposed

varmints......pests

humbly......not proud

nuzzled......pushed gently with the nose, cuddled

intrusion......enter without permission

guardianship......the act of taking care of another

Epilogue

perpetual......everlasting, endless

pooka......a mythical creature of Celtic folklore

About the Illustrator

Sharon Pape has been painting in oil and watercolor for 4 years, and while she has won numerous awards for her watercolor paintings of the animals she loves, this is her first time illustrating a book. She and her husband live outside of Albany, New York, near to her two married children and four grandchildren, who she enjoys spending time with and encouraging to be artistic in their own ways. Sharon can't wait to retire so she can spend more time painting. You can contact her by email at SharonPape@aol.com.

John and Mary Granato in their home at High Meadow

ABOUT THE AUTHOR

Mary Stewart Granato was born in upstate New York where she had the good fortune to grow up on the family farm which remained active until she was ten.

She received her Bachelor and Master degrees from the SUNY at Potsdam and from there entered into a teaching career which spanned 29 years at the elementary level. After retiring, she and her husband built their present home on a hill which they named High Meadow, a place so perfect that even the mosquitoes behave themselves.

<u>Tails of High Meadows- An Autumn Adventure</u> is her first book.

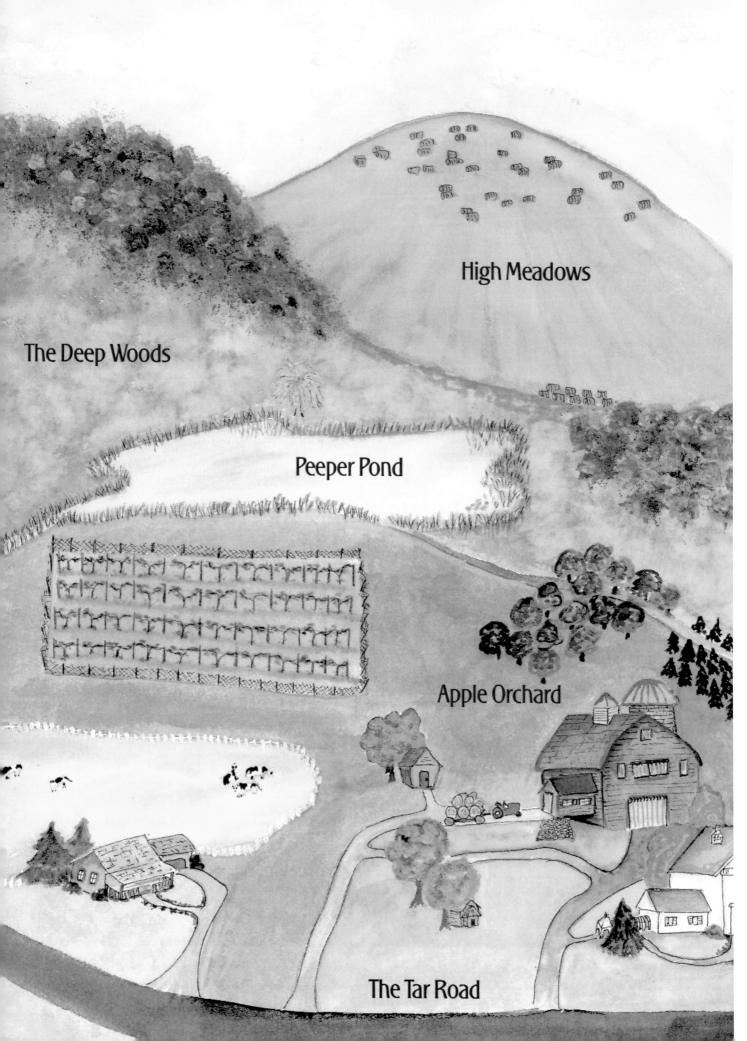